County Library

at Pearl Palace

For Princess Gayathri,
with love
VF
With special thanks to JD

www.tiaraclub.co.uk

ORCHARD BOOKS
338 Euston Road, London NW1 3BH
Orchard Books Australia
Level 17/207 Kent St, Sydney, NSW 2000
A Paperback Original
First published in 2007 by Orchard Books
Text © Vivian French 2007
Cover illustration © Sarah Gibb 2007
Inside illustrations © Orchard Books 2007

The right of Vivian French to be identified as the author
of this work has been asserted by her in accordance with the
Copyright, Designs and Patents Act, 1988.

A CIP catalogue record for this book is available
from the British Library.

ISBN 978 1 84616 500 9

1 3 5 7 9 10 8 6 4 2

Printed in Great Britain

The paper and board used in this paperback are natural recyclable
products made from wood grown in sustainable forests.
The manufacturing processes conform to the environmental
regulations of the country of origin.

Orchard Books is a division of Hachette Children's Books.
an Hachette Livre UK company.

www.orchardbooks.co.uk

The Tiara Club
at Pearl Palace

Princess Lucy

and the **Precious Puppy**

By Vivian French

ORCHARD BOOKS

The Royal Palace Academy
for the Preparation of Perfect Princesses

(Known to our students as "*The Princess Academy*")

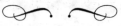

OUR SCHOOL MOTTO:
A Perfect Princess always thinks of others
before herself, and is kind, caring and truthful.

Pearl Palace offers a complete education for Tiara Club princesses with emphasis on the arts and outdoor activities. The curriculum includes:

A special Princess Sports Day

A trip to the Magical Mountains

Preparation for the Silver Swan Award (stories and poems)

A visit to the King Rudolfo's Exhibition of Musical Instruments

Our headteacher, King Everest, is present at all times, and students are well looked after by the head fairy godmother, Fairy G, and her assistant, Fairy Angora.

Our resident staff and visiting experts include:

QUEEN MOLLY (Sports and games)

LADY MALVEENA (Secretary to King Everest)

LORD HENRY (Natural History)

QUEEN MOTHER MATILDA (Etiquette, Posture and Flower Arranging)

We award tiara points to encourage our Tiara Club princesses towards the next level. All princesses who win enough points at Pearl Palace will be presented with their Pearl Sashes and attend a celebration ball.

Pearl Sash Tiara Club princesses are invited to go on to Emerald Castle, our very special residence for Perfect Princesses, where they may continue their education at a higher level.

PLEASE NOTE:
Pets are not allowed at Pearl Palace.
Princesses are expected to arrive at
the Academy with a *minimum* of:

Twenty ballgowns
*(with all necessary hoops,
petticoats, etc)*

Twelve day dresses

Seven gowns
*suitable for garden parties,
and other special
day occasions*

Twelve tiaras

Dancing shoes
five pairs

Velvet slippers
three pairs

Riding boots
two pairs

*Cloaks, muffs, stoles, gloves
and other essential
accessories as required*

Hi! I'm Princess Lucy, and I'm one
of the Lily Room princesses – and
I'm so very pleased you're here too.
You really are a Perfect Princess –
not like Diamonde and Gruella.
I'm lucky I've got you as a friend –
and I know Hannah, Isabella, Grace,
Ellie and Sarah think so too.
And I REALLY need my friends
when it's time for Sports Day...

Chapter One

Do you like games and PE? Don't tell anyone, but whenever someone throws a ball in my direction I just want to duck. Isn't that pathetic? But somehow I can't help it. And I can't jump, and I fall over when I try to run. I'm useless!

Luckily we've always had Fairy G

or Fairy Angora (our two fabulous school fairy godmothers) taking us for games, and they just laugh when I drop the ball, or fall over my feet. But at Pearl Palace we had a different games teacher, and she was SO enthusiastic.

It wasn't very princessy of us, but when we were on our own in Lily Room we called her Jolly Molly. We all liked her, but if I'm truthful I found her totally exhausting. She was always shouting "Watch the ball!" or trying to make me run faster. When I fell over she made me get up and run about some more, but it didn't make me any better at games. In fact as the time for the Pearl Palace Sports Day competition grew nearer and nearer I got worse and worse. Then we had a practice morning, and I dropped my egg in the egg and spoon race, tripped over all the hurdles, and came last by miles in the long jump.

"Princess Lucy," Queen Molly said, and she sounded horribly fierce, "please come and see me in my study at the end of the afternoon!"

I worried about what she was going to say all through Maths for the Modern Monarch, even though Sarah and Ellie and the rest of Lily Room did their best to cheer me up.

"Honestly, Lucy, it'll be fine," Hannah said as we packed up our maths books at the end of the afternoon. "She's probably going to give you extra lessons, or something like that."

"Do you want us to come with you?" Isabella asked.

"Maybe you could wait for me in the corridor," I said gratefully.

Queen Molly's study was at the other end of the building, and as we got nearer and nearer I felt more and more nervous. What if she'd decided to give me loads of minus tiara points? It would be SO dreadful if she did, because I knew Hannah was really hoping that Lily Room would win the competition, and I also knew I'd let everybody down however hard I tried. By the time I knocked on Queen Molly's door my hands were shaking.

"Come in!" she called, and I opened the door. "'Perfect Princesses are brave in ALL circumstances,'" I muttered to myself as I walked in, and then I stopped – and stared! The sweetest little rolypoly puppy was curled up in a basket beside Queen Molly's desk.

"Ah! Princess Lucy!" Queen Molly said. "Thank you so much for coming." She saw me looking at the puppy, and smiled. "That's Dexter. I'm looking after him for my mother – isn't he adorable?"

"He's GORGEOUS!" I said.

"He can be quite naughty," Queen Molly told me. "He's at his best when he's asleep. Now, I'm expecting another couple of princesses to join us, so shall we have a glass of orange juice while we're waiting?"

This was SO not what I'd expected that I couldn't answer for a moment. Then I nodded.

"Thank you very much, Your Majesty."

"Don't look so worried!" Queen Molly said. "I only wanted to talk to you about the competition."

"Oh," I said, and butterflies began to dance in my stomach again. "I'm...I'm sorry I'm so useless."

"That's all right." Queen Molly leant across and patted my arm. "I think—" but she was interrupted by a knock on the door.

"Come in!" she called, and to my amazement in walked the horrible twins, Diamonde and Gruella. When they saw me Diamonde made a face.

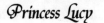
"What are YOU doing here, Lucy?" she hissed. "Queen Molly told us she had something special for us to do – she didn't say you'd be here. Or are you in trouble?"

Chapter Two

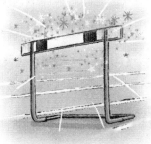

Before I could answer, Queen Molly sat down, and began to speak.

"Now, princesses," she said. "As you know, Sports Day is at the end of this week." She picked up several sheets of paper, and waved them at us. "There will be five events: the long jump, the high jump, the egg and spoon race, the hurdles, and finally the one hundred yards race. Marks will be given for each, and the team with the highest marks will win the competition and the Pearl Palace Trophy."

The butterflies in my stomach did triple loops, and my hands began to tremble again. Lily Room would NEVER win with me on the team. But then Queen Molly smiled at me, and put the papers down. "I've noticed that all three of you find games difficult, so I have something to suggest."

Diamonde tossed her head. "Mummy says Perfect Princesses don't need to be good at running about."

"And she says jumping hurdles gives you thick ankles," Gruella added.

Queen Molly began to laugh.

"That's SUCH nonsense, Gruella! Goodness – is that why you never make any effort? At least Lucy always tries her best."

I suddenly felt loads better, even though Diamonde and Gruella were glowering at me.

"Now," Queen Molly went on, "I'll need lots of help on Sports Day, so I thought I'd ask if you would be interested?"

"You mean we wouldn't have to take part in the competition?" I asked breathlessly. "Oh – yes PLEASE!"

Queen Molly smiled at me. "Excellent." She turned to the

twins. "What do you two think?"

Diamonde looked very doubtful. "What would we have to do?"

"Mummy wouldn't want us to do anything that wasn't suitable for Perfect Princesses," Gruella explained.

"Goodness, Gruella!" Queen Molly sounded annoyed. "Do you really think I would ask you to do something unsuitable? King Everest will be adding up the final tiara points, and I'll need you as messengers. Now, do you want to help, or not?"

"But what about OUR tiara points?" Diamonde wanted to

know. "It says on the Sports Day notice that 'princesses will receive tiara points for both skill and effort'. If we're just messengers we won't get points like everyone else."

I could tell Queen Molly was getting fed up with Diamonde. There was a frosty look in her eye

as she said, "If you try very hard to be helpful, Diamonde, of course you too will be rewarded with tiara points. Equally—" Queen Molly looked even frostier – "if you do NOT try, you will be given minus points."

Diamonde tossed back her blonde curls. "Mummy says Gruella and I make any event more memorable," she boasted. "We'll help."

"That's settled then." Queen Molly stood up. "The three of you will meet me by the long jump at the beginning of the competition, and I'll tell you what to do."

We curtsied, and thanked her. As we walked out into the corridor I saw Diamonde nudge Gruella.

"I bet loopy Lily Room think they're going to win," she whispered, but so loudly that I could still hear her. "We'll have to see about that!" And the two of them fell about laughing before they set off down the corridor.

Chapter Three

I hurried the other way, and found my friends waiting for me as they'd promised.

"You look a lot more cheerful," Grace said. "What did Jolly Molly say?"

"It's BRILLIANT!" I told her. "I'm going to be a helper on Sports Day, and I can win tiara points for being helpful instead of getting minus ones for falling over. Maybe Lily Room will win the competition now!"

"Well done, Lucy!" Hannah gave me a big hug. "Lily Room for ever! Let's go and practise!"

"Guess what?" I told her as we trooped outside. "Queen Molly's got the dearest little puppy in her room. She's looking after him for her mother, and she says he's very naughty!"

"Isn't King Everest allergic to dogs?" Grace asked.

I shook my head. "I don't know. I think it's only cats that make him sneeze. And I'm sure Queen Molly must have asked him if it's OK to have Dexter here."

"Dexter? Is that his name?" Sarah's eyes were shining. "That's so sweet. I wonder if she'd let us take him for a walk?"

31

Hannah pulled a stopwatch out of her pocket. "No time for walks at the moment! We've got to practice!"

By suppertime we were SO exhausted – even me, and all I'd been doing was check the watch. We staggered into the recreation room and flopped onto a sofa.

"Ooooh!" said a sneering voice from the other side of the room. "The loopy lilies have been running about, have they? Look how hot and puffed they are, Gruella. Did you ever see a Perfect Princess with a bright red face?"

"Never," Gruella giggled.

"Do you know what?" Hannah frowned at the twins. "Perfect Princesses never make fun of others, either!"

"Come on," I said quickly. "Let's go upstairs and change for supper."

After changing our clothes, we met Fairy G coming down the stairs. She was carrying a heap of golden lace, and she beamed at us.

"Very special decorations!" she boomed cheerfully. "Golden lace, and white satin! Should look lovely!"

"What's it for?" Sarah asked.

Fairy G leant against the

banister. "You mean you don't know about the ball?"

When we shook our heads, she began to chuckle. "It's King Everest's treat for you, my dears. He's decided to have a Sports Day Ball." She gave us a little wink. "I think he thinks that's funny."

We looked at each other, and we were all smiling the most enormous smiles.

"It's AGES since we had a ball," Grace said. "I was wondering if I'd ever wear my ballgown again!"

"Will it be in the evening of Sports Day, Fairy G?" Ellie wanted to know.

Fairy G nodded. "Indeed it will, my dears. And King Everest will announce the winners just before the music begins." She beamed again, and thumped off down the stairs singing "Tra la la!" as she went.

Chapter Four

On the morning of Pearl Palace Sports Day I woke to find my friends already up and dressed.

"What's going on?" I asked sleepily.

"We're all horribly nervous," Isabella said. "I'm absolutely sure I'm going to trip over every single hurdle."

"You won't," I told her. "You're BRILLIANT! Last time we practised you were perfect!"

"But loads of people will be watching today." Ellie grabbed my arm. "I KNOW I'm going to drop my egg in the egg and spoon race!"

I squeezed her hand. "It'll be fine – truly it will."

Sarah sighed. "I know a Perfect Princess shouldn't really mind if she comes first or last, but I WOULD like Lily Room to win..."

"Let's go and have some breakfast," I suggested. "You'll feel loads better afterwards."

But when we got to the dining hall none of us could eat much. I didn't like to say anything, but I was feeling nervous too, and by the time we trooped out onto the games field we were all shaking.

It didn't help that it looked
so grand – there were flags
everywhere, and shiny balloons
bobbing on the end of long strings,
and a ginormous flowery arch at
the end of the running track.

Queen Molly was rushing about looking flustered, Lady Malveena was hurrying here and there with handfuls of lists, and Queen Mother Matilda was holding a megaphone and looking cross.

"Excuse me!" she called out. "WHEN do you want me to announce the first event?"

"We begin at ten o'clock exactly, Your Majesty." Lady Malveena was as cool as a cucumber.

Queen Molly saw me, and waved. "Princess Lucy – I need you!"

I hurried towards her. "Yes, Your Majesty?"

"Something rather awkward has happened!" Queen Molly looked anxiously over her shoulder, and beckoned me closer. "You remember Dexter? My mother's precious puppy?"

"Oh YES!" I said.

"Well—" Queen Molly began to whisper, "he must have slipped out of my door this morning. I can't find him anywhere! And I haven't got time to look for him. Could you be an angel and see if you can find him?" She rubbed her ear, and I could see she was embarrassed. "I'm SO sorry to ask you – because it means I won't be able to give you any tiara points for taking messages. You see—" she went very red – "King Everest doesn't actually know Dexter's here. I'm only looking after him for a week, so I haven't mentioned it... Oh dear. I feel DREADFUL asking you to help me!"

I stood up very straight. All kinds of thoughts were whizzing round inside my head, but I told myself that Perfect Princesses always answer a call for help. "Don't worry, Queen Molly,"

I said. "I'll do my very best to find him for you."

As I hurried back towards Pearl Palace I saw Diamonde and Gruella walking towards me.

Their heads were close together, and I heard Gruella say, "I let him out, like you told me to, but he ran off..."

"SH!" Diamonde hissed as she saw me. She pretended to smile. "Aren't we meant to be meeting Queen Molly, Lucy?"

"There's something I've got to do in school first," I said, and I dashed on past them – and all but crashed into our headteacher.

"Princess Lucy!" King Everest didn't look very pleased. "May I ask WHY you are running in the WRONG direction?"

"Erm...if you please, Your Majesty, I've..." It was awful! I couldn't think of a single excuse. I gulped. "Erm...I've left my running shoes in my room."

King Everest frowned. "Five minus tiara points," he said. "I shall expect you back on the games field in two minutes!"

"Yes, Your Majesty!" I bobbed the quickest curtsey ever, and fled...hoping desperately that the king wouldn't notice I was already wearing my running shoes.

Chapter Five

As I reached the school buildings I heard Queen Mum Mattie's voice booming through the megaphone.

"Please take your places for the long jump!"

I crossed my fingers for Sarah and the others, opened the door – and Dexter hurled himself against my legs, yapping and jumping up at me as if he was my very best friend ever.

"DEXTER!" I gasped, and made a grab for his collar. My fingers actually touched it – but then he was off, leaping about just out of my reach.

"Good dog!" I said. "Good boy!
Come here, there's a good puppy!"

But he didn't. If I went towards
him he bounced backwards. If
I went backwards he danced
towards me – but never near
enough to be caught.

"Maybe I can get him back inside?" I thought, but that didn't work either. Dexter just sat down with a catch-me-if-you-can expression on his face.

I decided I'd have to be very cunning, so I sat on the doorstep and began to talk to him in my quietest voice. Gradually, little by little, he edged closer. It took AGES; I heard Queen Mum Mattie announce the high jump, the egg and spoon race, and then the hurdles, and Dexter was still not quite near enough to catch.

"GOOD puppy," I crooned, "GOOD puppy..." and he actually

sniffed my fingers. "One step more, and I'll be able to catch him," I told myself. "GOOD pup—"

CRASH!

I don't know what they dropped in the school kitchen, but it sounded like a million plates at once. Dexter was off like a shot, and I took off after him. I HAD to see where he was going – what would happen if I lost sight of him? I fixed my eyes on Dexter's little wagging tail and ran like

I've never ever run before. I was vaguely conscious of people shouting and screaming as Dexter charged through groups of princesses and kings and queens, but I couldn't stop to see what or who he'd upset. I just followed him, terrified that he'd disappear into the distance and I'd never see him again.

On and on we ran – and I suddenly noticed there were people running beside me, and loud cheering instead of shouting. On I went, my heart hammering inside me – and suddenly Fairy G stepped out in front of me, and waved her wand.

"Yip yip YIP!" Dexter flew in

the air, did a double somersault in
the middle of a cloud of stars –
and landed safe in Queen Molly's
arms. I was running so fast
I couldn't stop...and when I did
I couldn't breathe. I doubled up to
try and catch my breath, and for
the first time I looked round – and
I couldn't believe what I saw.

I was at the end of the race track – and there were crowds of princesses cheering wildly on either side!

Hannah, Isabella, Grace, Ellie and Sarah appeared beside me and hugged me – and told me I'd won.

"WHAT?" I gasped.

"You've WON, Lucy – you've WON!"

I couldn't believe my ears.

I'd actually won the one hundred metres race!

But then I thought, actually, I hadn't. It was Dexter who'd won. When I finally got my breath back I saw Queen Molly was holding him tightly, and was talking earnestly to King Everest. Then she turned, and pointed at me.

"Oh NO," I thought. "We'll be in such trouble now!"

But we weren't. King Everest began to laugh, and he laughed so loudly Dexter began to yap and wriggle as if he was laughing too.

"Princess Lucy!" King Everest called, "please come here!"

I walked towards him, blushing madly.

"Helping Queen Molly hide her guilty secret was a very terrible thing to do, Princess Lucy," the king said sternly, but there was such a twinkle in his eye I couldn't take him seriously.

"I'm very sorry, Your Majesty." I tried to sound as apologetic as I could, but it was difficult because he was twinkling more and more.

"Quite right!" He let out such a loud guffaw that it made me jump. "I've never seen a princess run like you did! Just to catch

a naughty little puppy!"

I stared at my feet. "Erm...I'm very fond of dogs," was all I could say.

"Well, I think you'd better help Queen Molly look after this puppy until his owner comes to collect him. In fact, you've done so well that I'm going to allow you to take him for a walk tomorrow morning instead of helping tidy up. Tell your friends from Lily Room they can come too, if you like. And I'll cancel those five minus tiara points I gave you just now. Does that sound fair?"

"Oh!" I curtsied my best curtsey ever. "THANK YOU, Your Majesty!"

King Everest nodded at me. "You'd better run along and get ready for the Sports Day ball. I'll see you there!"

Chapter Six

I got ready for the ball in a dream. My friends told me how utterly astonished they'd been when Dexter and I appeared at the start of the race track just as Queen Mother Matilda said "One, two, three, go!" They said I'd even beaten Charlotte from Rose Room – but I couldn't remember the race at all. All I could think about was how tired I was, and what fun it would be playing with Dexter in the morning...but when I walked into the grand ballroom I forgot all about being tired.

It was SO magnificent! Chandeliers hung sparkling from the ceiling, and the walls were covered in white satin and swathes of golden lace. King Everest's jewel-studded throne was placed on a high platform next to the musicians, and Fairy G, Fairy Angora and Queen Mother Matilda were already sitting on the stage.

As soon as the last princess had scurried in through the door the trumpeter played a fanfare, and King Everest strode in carrying a HUGE trophy.

"Well done! Well done! I'm pleased to announce that the Pearl

Palace Sports Day has been a great success!" he beamed. "Lots of records have been broken, and I think every princess who took part proved that she truly believes that 'A Perfect Princess does her best in every situation.'" Now, I'm

sure you're longing to know which team has won the competition. It was very, very close – in fact, until the final race all the teams had equal points. But then we had a surprise winner and she won so well that she tipped the balance. The winner of the Pearl Palace Sports Day competition is Lily Room – and I would like Princess Lucy to come and collect the trophy!"

I nearly died of shock. My friends were whooping and jumping about – and I could feel my legs wobbling as I stepped forward.

"Well done, Lucy, well done indeed!" King Everest said as he handed me the trophy.

"And now – three cheers for Lily Room! And let the Sports Day Ball begin!"

Was the ball fun?
It was GLORIOUS.

I managed to dance almost every dance, although by the end I was so tired I could hardly stagger up the stairs to bed. It was so lovely to curl up under my soft warm covers...and to know that the very next day I'd be taking Dexter out for a walk with my friends.

There's just one thing that would really make tomorrow COMPLETELY perfect...

And that's if you could come too...

What happens next?
Find out in

Princess Grace
and the Golden Nightingale

Hello, lovely princess.
I'm Princess Grace, and
I think you might have already
met Hannah, Isabella, Lucy, Ellie
and Sarah - we share Lily Room,
and it's wonderful! Just imagine
sharing with Diamonde and
Gruella - you'd probably find
toads in your shoes or spiders
in your slippers. Oooh!
Wouldn't that be AWFUL?

Look out for

Princess Parade

with Princess Hannah and Princess Lucy
ISBN 978 1 84616 504 7

*And look out for the Daffodil Room princesses in
the Tiara Club at Emerald Castle:*

Princess Amelia and the Silver Seal
Princess Leah and the Golden Seahorse
Princess Ruby and the Enchanted Whale
Princess Millie and the Magical Mermaid
Princess Rachel and the Dancing Dolphin
Princess Zoe and the Wishing Shell

Win a Tiara Club
Perfect Princess Prize!

Look for the secret word in mirror writing that is hidden in a tiara in each of the Tiara Club books. Each book has one word. Put together the six words from books **19** to **24** to make a special Perfect Princess sentence, then send it to us together with 20 words or more on why you like the Tiara Club books. Each month, we will put the correct entries in a draw and one lucky reader will receive a magical Perfect Princess prize!

Send your Perfect Princess sentence,
at least 20 words on why you like the Tiara Club,
your name and your address on a postcard to:
The Tiara Club Competition,
Orchard Books, 338 Euston Road,
London, NW1 3BH

Australian readers should write to:
Hachette Children's Books,
Level 17/207 Kent Street, Sydney, NSW 2000.

Only one entry per child.
Final draw: 30 September 2008

By Vivian French
Illustrated by Sarah Gibb

The Tiara Club

PRINCESS CHARLOTTE AND THE **BIRTHDAY BALL**	ISBN	978 1 84362 863 7
PRINCESS KATIE AND THE **SILVER PONY**	ISBN	978 1 84362 860 6
PRINCESS DAISY AND THE **DAZZLING DRAGON**	ISBN	978 1 84362 864 4
PRINCESS ALICE AND THE **MAGICAL MIRROR**	ISBN	978 1 84362 861 3
PRINCESS SOPHIA AND THE **SPARKLING SURPRISE**	ISBN	978 1 84362 862 0
PRINCESS EMILY AND THE **BEAUTIFUL FAIRY**	ISBN	978 1 84362 859 0

The Tiara Club at Silver Towers

PRINCESS CHARLOTTE AND THE **ENCHANTED ROSE**	ISBN	978 1 84616 195 7
PRINCESS KATIE AND THE **DANCING BROOM**	ISBN	978 1 84616 196 4
PRINCESS DAISY AND THE **MAGICAL MERRY-GO-ROUND**	ISBN	978 1 84616 197 1
PRINCESS ALICE AND THE **CRYSTAL SLIPPER**	ISBN	978 1 84616 198 8
PRINCESS SOPHIA AND THE **PRINCE'S PARTY**	ISBN	978 1 84616 199 5
PRINCESS EMILY AND THE **WISHING STAR**	ISBN	978 1 84616 200 8

The Tiara Club at Ruby Mansions

PRINCESS CHLOE AND THE **PRIMROSE PETTICOATS**	ISBN	978 1 84616 290 9
PRINCESS JESSICA AND THE **BEST-FRIEND BRACELET**	ISBN	978 1 84616 291 6
PRINCESS GEORGIA AND THE **SHIMMERING PEARL**	ISBN	978 1 84616 292 3
PRINCESS OLIVIA AND THE **VELVET CLOAK**	ISBN	978 1 84616 293 0
PRINCESS LAUREN AND THE **DIAMOND NECKLACE**	ISBN	978 1 84616 294 7
PRINCESS AMY AND THE **GOLDEN COACH**	ISBN	978 1 84616 295 4

The Tiara Club at Pearl Palace

PRINCESS HANNAH
AND THE LITTLE BLACK KITTEN   ISBN   978 1 84616 498 9

PRINCESS ISABELLA
AND THE SNOW-WHITE UNICORN   ISBN   978 1 84616 499 6

PRINCESS LUCY
AND THE PRECIOUS PUPPY   ISBN   978 1 84616 500 9

PRINCESS GRACE
AND THE GOLDEN NIGHTINGALE   ISBN   978 1 84616 501 6

PRINCESS ELLIE
AND THE ENCHANTED FAWN   ISBN   978 1 84616 502 3

PRINCESS SARAH
AND THE SILVER SWAN   ISBN   978 1 84616 503 0

BUTTERFLY BALL   ISBN   978 1 84616 470 5

CHRISTMAS WONDERLAND   ISBN   978 1 84616 296 1

PRINCESS PARADE   ISBN   978 1 84616 504 7

All priced at £3.99.
Butterfly Ball, Christmas Wonderland and *Princess Parade* are priced at £5.99.
The Tiara Club books are available from all good bookshops, or can be ordered
direct from the publisher: Orchard Books, PO BOX 29, Douglas IM99 IBQ.
Credit card orders please telephone 01624 836000
or fax 01624 837033 or visit our website: www.orchardbooks.co.uk
or e-mail: bookshop@enterprise.net for details.

To order please quote title, author and ISBN and your full name and address.
Cheques and postal orders should be made payable to 'Bookpost plc.'
Postage and packing is FREE within the UK
(overseas customers should add £2.00 per book).

Prices and availability are subject to change.

Check out

The
Tiara
Club

website at:

www.tiaraclub.co.uk

You'll find Perfect Princess games and fun
things to do, as well as news on the Tiara
Club and all your favourite princesses!